Christmas Stories

From My Family to Yours

SUSANNE SIR

WESTBOW
PRESS®
A DIVISION OF THOMAS NELSON
& ZONDERVAN

WestBow Press books may be ordered through booksellers or by contacting:

WestBow Press
A Division of Thomas Nelson & Zondervan
1663 Liberty Drive
Bloomington, IN 47403
www.westbowpress.com
1 (866) 928-1240

ISBN: 978-1-9736-7432-0 (sc)
ISBN: 978-1-9736-7431-3 (e)

Library of Congress Control Number: 2019914183

Print information available on the last page.

WestBow Press rev. date: 10/9/2019

Previous Writings by Susanne Sir

Murder in the Shores / *A Georgi Girl Series*
The Fortune Cookie
We Clean Up
Six Hands
The Wheel of Misfortune

Warmth, Joy, and Love

To my sisters, Lita and Ellen, and my brothers, Nils and Albert, for the memories we have shared sitting around our Christmas tree on Christmas Eve!

To my stars—Greta, Annie, Ripper, Toni, Tori, Teel, SuSu, and Dee. Thank you for sharing!

All who call on God in true faith, earnestly from the heart, will certainly be heard, and will receive what they have asked and desired, although not in the hour or in the measure, or the very thing which they asked; yet they will obtain something greater and more glorious than they had dared to ask.

—Martin Luther

Acknowledgments

To the esteemed WestBow Press for publishing my humble work. Thank you!

To Eric Schroeder of WestBow Press who has provided encouragement, wisdom, guidance, and friendship. You are valued.

Introduction

How did *Christmas Stories* get to be written? Anyone could do a card. I found the Christmas letter to be tedious. It is difficult to stay focused on Johnnie's braces, if you know what I mean. But along came an adorably true story with an animal at the center. So I wrote about the adventure and added a few things from my vivid imagination. The stories were always tied to God's love.

I sent out the first story at Christmastime in lieu of a card or letter. Many encouraging reviews filtered down to me. Teachers shared the story with their pupils. Parents read the stories to their children. My field of sharing was growing. Each year a new animal story happened.

But one year someone's mail was displaced. I received an angry email about the missing famous "Christmas story." Where did the *famous* come from?

This is when I realized the importance of the Christmas story to those who received it. I buckled down and continued to look for that special story each year. I now had accumulated quite a few. What was fun was the fact that most of the stories are true.

I have two exceptions to this, as they are actually fiction. The first was about a little girl who had fallen in love with a turtle in our home. Every time she saw me, she would ask, "Has anyone brought you a baby turtle?"

I had explained to her that this had happened to us quite often. My answer to her was, "No, there are not any new baby turtles."

As it drew near to Christmas, I decided I had to buy a turtle and give it to her. I then realized it would not seem right to tell her I bought the turtle. What would her parents think? Somehow it would not be as much fun. So I created the story, "Lucky, the Falling Star." I hope you enjoy reading it.

I created the second fiction piece to generate another possible series. I am the author of *Murder in the Shores / A Georgi Girl Series*. I had invested a lot of time in this new series creation and decided to also make it my Christmas story for that year. It is "My View Is Sunny," and I hope you enjoy this story as well.

All the animals are not from my imagination but are God's creation. I decided these works of love for my family needed to be shared with other families, neighbors, and friends. I have signed the letters as I would have when sending them at Christmastime.

Enjoy! Maybe you have a story you would like to share!

In God's love,
Susanne

List of Characters

Susanne, myself

George, my husband

Annie, a red cocker spaniel

Ripper, a baby parrot

Toni, a Florida box turtle

Teel, an African spurred tortoise

Tori, a gopher tortoise

SuSu, a chocolate-brown cocker spaniel

Dee, a dove

Snooty, the neighbor's cat

Sunny, the bag lady

Tiny, a baby turtle

Baby, a mockingbird

Gandy, one of four Egyptian baby geese

Ugly, a duck

Lucky, a baby red slider turtle

Tiny Coot, a Florida baby coot

And last but not least, Greta, our goose

Two Sides to a Story

Last Christmas our family (and our dog Spitfire too) visited a reenactment of Dade's Massacre, which took place on December 28, 1835. A dispute between the Government of the United States and the Seminole over the right of the later to occupy land in Florida. Frank Latimer, author of *Dade's Last Command*, had invited us as guests. This reenactment was held in Bushnell, Florida.

It was an outstanding professional performance. Both the actors playing the soldiers and those playing the Indians took pride in the authenticity of their uniforms and campsites, which they were judged on this. Horses, cannons, rifle fire, and even tree cutting brought us back into this time and battle.

The most enlightening was Frank Latimer's narration for the soldiers and Tiger Tail for the Native Americans. There was rightness to both sides. If only they had been able to find a better way to settle their differences.

The town of Bushnell was just as interesting. It reminded us of times past. There were cattle grazing and many churches, and quiet streets, but all at a slower pace. It was a look back in time of family values and great childhoods.

We hope that you have a meaningful holiday with beautiful memories of previous, slower-paced Christmases with your loved ones.

Merry Christmas,
Susanne, George, Ripper, and Annie (a.k.a. "Spitfire")

P.S. Ripper is our baby parrot. The metermen are terrified of him. His screech is frightening, and he is fearless. Even though he is small, he drives our cocker spaniel, Annie, crazy. Annie had to be placed on a diet. It was too much of the good dog's life.

Thank God for Tiny Miracles

Christmas 2005

It was a beautiful day in May. George and Annie were out for their morning walk. Annie had her nose to the ground as usual. George noticed Annie cautiously inspecting something small on the sidewalk. Upon further observation, he saw it was a newly born water turtle. It was very far from the water for its short time in this big world, and George noticed its tiny feet. We named it Tiny.

It appeared a bird had picked Tiny up in its bill after he or she hatched and took it to an area for consumption. Shortly before George and Annie came upon Tiny, it must have gotten loose from the bird's bill and landed on the grass close to the sidewalk. It then made its way out to the sidewalk. Now some people would say this was chance or luck. I say this was God's will for a tiny miracle.

Tiny is doing well. He is getting big and soon will be ready to be out in the world on his own. There comes a time when the little one grows up and is ready to leave the nest, so to speak. And this is the case with Tiny.

But George kept procrastinating. Tiny wasn't ready yet to handle the world on its own. He needed a little more time to grow. But eventually George ran out of excuses, and the day arrived.

The send-off took place from our lake steps. George and Annie watched Tiny take to the lake, just like a big turtle. They were sad to see Tiny go, but the turtle was delighted with no more rules or confining walls.

"I am free to do as I please and to feel my wings and fly—only in this case to paddle," you could practically hear Tiny say.

Tiny met other turtles who became his friends, and together they found food and shelter. Occasionally we'd see a little turtle head above the waterline watching the house, and we knew it was Tiny.

3

Such is life with our children. God has taught us love through his example. God loves all his children, and offers us security, trust, and eternal forgiveness. He is our safe haven and our protector. We hope you are also enjoying God's tiny miracles.

Susanne, George, Annie, Ripper, Toni, and Teel

P.S. Did you notice a new addition? We received a call from a lake neighbor. He found a turtle swimming frantically toward his dock. (They are not swimmers, so the word *frantic* would be true.) The neighbor turned the turtle over to us, and he was duly named after his rescuing benefactor. We have had a turtle crawl made with a little pond and house with a palm roof. We now have Teel enjoying the turtle crawl.

Also, an endangered animal, a Florida box turtle, was born on our property. George retrieved her from the path of any danger and brought her inside to grow in safety. We named the turtle Toni, and we are official protectors of this turtle.

Let There Be Peace and Goodwill to All Feathered Friends on the Lake

Christmas 2006

On December 1 when I arrived home, I found a new addition swimming on our lake. George rushed out to tell me about the new arrival, but it was hardly necessary. This loud grating sound was coming from our tranquil lake. The only way I can describe the sound is to say it is like the bleat of a lamb, but on a higher note and very loud. Of course I am no expert on these sounds. I followed the sound waves, and there in all her beauty was a huge and beautiful goose.

The goose continued to bleat for days. I noticed across the lake that she had set up her quarters on a neighbor's shoreline. In desperation, the neighbor started to prune this area, which naturally sent the bleating goose to someone else's shoreline.

I thought, *This is not looking too good for Goosy. The neighbors would start complaining, and this could lead to "Goosy be gone."*

Then, in true fashion for the season, Goosy's prayers were answered. Fortunately for Goosy, God was listening. Personally, I would not have the foggiest idea what a goose would pray about.

So as this story goes, another new arrival landed. Instead of beauty, this time the arrival was one of the ugliest ducks I have ever seen. As they say, "beauty is in the eye of the beholder." This duck was beautiful to the gorgeous goose. They became immediate buddies, swimming together with their paddle feet, fluffing their feathers, and wagging their tails. This must be duck-and-goose fun. They were also both able to fly, although Goosy was more of a bomber, version due to her size. Like an aircraft carrier. Wherever Ducky went, Goosy followed.

Goosy stopped bleating the blues. That soulful sound was from loneliness. Goosy needed a friend. Goosy did not care what color, sex, age, appearance, species, or religion that Ducky was. There was no prejudice here. Goosy was just happy to have a friend, and that friend was beautiful in her eyes.

What a Christmas message was sent to all of us who witnessed this heartwarming act. God wishes us to see beauty in all his creation and live in peace. At least cut down on the bleating and have a silent night!

Susanne, George, Greta, Toni, Teel, Annie, and Ripper

God's Family

Christmas 2007

It was a picture-perfect Florida day—blue sky, fluffy white clouds, and low humidity. It doesn't get any better than that. It was early December, and George and Annie were out for a walk, enjoying all those great smells that only doggies like. And then Annie's nose came upon something really special.

George was trying to encourage Annie to move along, but you cannot budge her when she gets determined. (She's a muscle dog.) George took a closer look at what was holding things up. There on the curb lawn was a very small baby bird, a mockingbird. In the flash of a moment, the hunter in Annie secured the bird in her mouth without hurting it.

At this time, Mom and Dad Birdie spotted their baby. Not happy with this situation, they decided to attack Annie's back end. Now most dogs wouldn't have liked this and would have dropped their catch. But not Spitfire. This dog had a mission. She would have made a great missionary dog, if there were such a thing. She's like another Lassie, only shorter.

Of course, George was also under their attack, as the mockingbird parents were buzzing around his head and going in for dives toward him. Thank goodness he was wearing a hat, or it could have affected his hair growth. Now that I think of it, there is little or no chance of that happening since his head is shaven.

George, Annie, and Mocker's parents proceeded very quickly to the garage, where George found a small box with low sides. Once the baby bird was retrieved from Annie, who appeared to have gotten lockjaw, it was put in the box and placed near the cherry hedge, which is where it must have fallen from its nest.

Both Annie and George retreated to watch the great reunion. There's nothing like the love of Mr. and Mrs. Mocking for their baby mocking. I find God's love for us just as beautiful!

Susanne, George, Toni, Annie, Ripper, and Greta

P.S. Teel escaped from the turtle crawl.

Home Sweet Home

Christmas 2008

We have a new addition to our lake group, Tori, a gopher tortoise. A friend had heard that Tori was in danger. (She was busily creating tunnels all over a neighbor's backyard. Gopher tortoise love to burrow.) It was suggested that the friend capture the digger and deliver her to us.

A neighbor assisted in building a little shelter while his two children helped and placed palm leaves across the top to create a roof. George piled sand all around the base, and even added a little pond. Tori had to go uphill and down to enter her little paradise. This made her very happy.

We were having our house tented, and naturally we had to do something with Tori. The first idea George had was to put her in a neighbor's fenced-in yard—with their approval, of course.

So on the day of the tenting, Tori was placed in the neighbor's backyard. Shortly after Tory was placed there, George went outside and found her waiting outside her turtle crawl on our property. She was placed back in the neighbor's backyard two more times, both with the same result.

Tori may be Houdini or might have developed another underground tunnel system (popular in the Southern states), bringing her back home. She was then left outside with Annie while new plans were created. Tori immediately took a liking to Annie and with great speed. (Where does a turtle get speed, much less great?) She tried to catch up with Annie.

To Annie's concern, she could not shake Tori. Annie took to a flight of steps in desperation, and once at the top, she turned to see if the monster were still following. Tori was unable to go further. Quick thinking, Annie!

It was then decided to contact a private school in the area who had an animal shelter for their students, teaching them care and responsibility for animals in need. They graciously consented to take care of Tori.

In reflection, Tori's journey to return to her "home sweet home" is something we all do around this time of year. Our roots, family, friends, and neighbors who mean so much to us, we long to see and reunite with.

Let this Christmas be a "home sweet home" to you and your family, friends, and neighbors.

Susanne, George, Toni, Annie, Ripper, and Greta

Thank God There Were Four

Christmas 2009

We found Tami, our neighbor, chasing a baby goose in our backyard. George joined in, and she pointed to the lake where three other baby geese were swimming close by. Tami caught the escapee and put it back in the lake to join its brothers and sisters. Then, as she was leaving, she mentioned that she hadn't seen Madre and Padre Goose. Upon reflection, I recalled a huge fight several days ago with the Egyptian geese.

Later that day George witnessed one of the orphans swimming over to a duck, thinking it must be Mom. Life can be cruel. The supposed mom turned out to be an impostor and proceeded to swim away. The baby goose was not near the shore and could not keep up. Originally there were four. Now there were three.

We heard chirping all night from the "Three Musketeers." By morning our minds were made up that we needed to save them. Tami couldn't sleep either. The whole lake neighborhood must have tossed and turned all night. Tami awoke, determined to save these little geese in distress. As the most agile neighbor, she caught all three with cheers from the rest of us.

George raced to the nearest feed store for food and the proper cage that would be both large and secure. Almost immediately after being placed in the cage, one died. Possibly it was shock. Overnight we lost another. Thankfully the struggle to survive prevailed, and then there was one: Gandy (a.k.a. Little Hulk).

Through trial and error, we learned the right amounts of water and food that Gandy liked. Neighbors stopped by to check on the lucky goose as word got out. Then one day a lone male Egyptian goose showed up. It cocked its head toward the garage and heard the chirping. We thought, *this must be Dad returned to help its baby.*

We got some cooler weather and added a heat lamp to the baby goose's cage.

Gandy was becoming huge, but not big enough to be released. Of course the older male goose was even bigger and had a huge chest.

One morning George was a little careless and did not properly secure the cage door. Gandy seized the opportunity to escape, but he soon learned it was not a good move. As Gandy took off in the yard, Big Bully (the dad or supposed dad) took off after it and bit the baby.

George heard the commotion and quickly joined in the chase. First place was Little Hulk. Second place was Big Bully. And bringing up the rear was George. George really was fast! The race continued. Then Big Bully tripped. Little Hulk paused, and George moved in and recovered Little Hulk, who went meekly back to his cage.

It was now apparent Big Bully was not Dada, and we could not release Gandy back into the lake.

We contacted the Pelican Seabird Station, who agreed to accept and care for Little Hulk. Parting was rough for the neighbors and us. The rescue center also located a goose of the same age in another county. They drove Gandy to that location so they could both grow up together. Maybe a cousin?

Babies are adorable and normally bring out the best in all of us. This is the season for Christ's birth. Let us rejoice in the joy that Christ's birth brings us, and let the love shine through to make us better neighbors, friends, and family members.

Merry Christmas!

Susanne, George, Greta, Toni, Annie, and Ripper

The Ugly Duck Came Home for Christmas: God Loves All His Creation

Christmas 2010

eorge related the afternoon events to me when I got home. Upon pulling in the garage, George had noticed the ugly duck was actually on the front portion of the property. George has this thing that Ducky is not good enough for Goosy. So like any father with a fancy-free goose, he silently approached the gate to the backyard and closed it. Now with a smile on his face and a lighter step to his stride, he proceeded with his yard duties. He may even have been whistling.

Now Ducky waddled a little heavier with wings hanging down in depression. Knowing he was shut out of the backyard, he started to inspect his new surroundings. Ahead was the street with large, moving metal objects, but to his left was inviting grass and shrubs. So he went to his left. Upon getting to the end of the lawn, he could not go any further due to the hedge. So again he had a choice and went to the left.

As the old Chinese proverb goes, "Young ducks do not go to the west. Go to the left." As his eyes looked down the sloping lawn, he thought he saw George on the other side of the fence. Yes, he was sure it was George, and just at that moment, George looked up and saw Ducky.

Ducky was now excited. He knew what to do, so he fluffed his feathers and sauntered down the slope with a quick waddle. He could see the expression on George's face change from surprise to horror. George also started to wave his arms frantically.

Ducky thought, *He must be happy to see me. Nice guy!*

Ducky was just about to the fence now. He opened his wings and flew to the top of the fence, paused, and leapfrogged—excuse me, I meant leap-ducked—to the top of George's head. George was still waving his arms and staggering around with Ducky hanging onto his head.

Ducky thought, *this is almost as good as a buoy ride.*

Then he saw Greta, his beautiful goose friend. She had her beak pulled back in a smile. The ugly duck smiled too and jumped off "George buoy" to join her. George was also now feeling better.

The lesson is even if your initial idea were wrong, you can always change its path into something good. Tis the season for good works!

We wish you all good things, health, and happiness.

From the Lake Gang,
Susanne, George, Annie, Toni, Greta, and Ducky

P.S. Ripper has left the Lake Gang this year. God has flown him to heaven for the good life.

Do Unto Geese As You Would Have Geese Do Unto You: The Golden Goose Rule

Christmas 2011

It was around 8:00 p.m. when our front doorbell rang. Taking a quick safety look through our peephole, I did not recognize the couple standing at our door. Upon opening, the Bakers very politely introduced themselves as neighbors living several blocks away. A very handsome couple, they were looking for the owners of a goose that they had found in their yard when they had returned home from work tonight. Their neighbors had told them that the goose had spent the day in the neighborhood. She was enjoyed by all.

The Bakers knew of our lake and figured this would be her home. Yes, we had missed Greta, and she was our goose. We arranged that they would return Greta in the morning since it was already dark and she was secured by fence at their property for the night.

The next morning Mrs. Baker and her mom walked Greta to a busy cross street, and to everyone's amazement, Greta stood waiting with Mrs. Baker while traffic came to a halt. Greta displayed an attitude of, "This is how it should be, although I have never seen a goose-crossing sign."

She calmly and slowly proceeded to waddle across the street. Greta is no fool. She was going to enjoy her fifteen minutes of fame and hope pictures were being taken. When she saw the lake, she waddled faster and jumped in with a happy tail-wagging dance.

Later that day George happened to be walking Annie and noticed Greta on the curb lawn, very close to the road. He was naturally concerned for her safety. He ordered her to get to the backyard.

A passing neighbor and his dog both stood in astonishment, as they watched the goose understand the command and immediately fast-waddle to the driveway and down to the backyard.

A few days later, George again found her close to the road and busy traffic. Is this a situation where the grass is greener out front? Anyway, this time Greta decided to have some fun and played "Ring Around the Rosie" with George and our car in the driveway. It was amusing for all except George to watch. George was worn out from the chase. Greta, finally tired of the game, headed to the backyard.

I happened to be enjoying a cup of coffee, and I looked out our window and saw John, our next-door neighbor, aiming his camera at Greta. She was curled up and sound asleep in our flower bed next to the Bobbing Bird, my pet name for this garden ornament shaped like a crane that swings around on a metal stand, bobbing up and down. Greta believes it is real and spends hours discussing the lake news with the Bobbing Bird. Occasionally when Greta's tail is facing the crane, the Bobbing Bird will peck it as it takes a dip down.

Greta, thinking this was intentional, quickly swung around to grab its beak for attacking her. The Bobbing Bird's tail and beak have been destroyed from these encounters with Greta. John was hoping to get one of these priceless pictures.

Greta is adorable and friendly. She needs our help but also brings us joy. It is that way with all of God's creatures. Reach out and touch someone and feel God's love.

Merry Christmas.

Susanne, George, Greta, Toni, and Annie

God's Glorious Gift

Christmas 2012

This year we lost our precious cocker spaniel, Annie. I expected to spend a long time grieving our loss, but life can be surprising and not predictable. Family, friends, and neighbors were extremely kind in helping us with our grief. One statement I kept hearing was, "Get another dog and give it a good home and love." This must have helped George. He started to look into the Humane Society and shelters for lost dogs. He finally reached out to a kennel in Sanibel, Florida, fairly close to home. Yes, they had a puppy, a show dog. Wow!

George couldn't wait to get there. As soon as he saw her, his comment was, "She is beautiful."

I suggested we go out to lunch and talk this over, but I knew in my heart that this little puppy was already in George's heart. And after a great lunch, we returned to the breeder.

"We are interested in the puppy," we both told her.

As we stood there before the breeder and the puppy, we realized we had gotten it wrong. The decision was not ours. George and I looked across at each other, sucked in our stomachs, squared off our shoulders, and tried to put our best foot forward. It seemed we stood there for an eternity. The breeder was watching the puppy, and the puppy was not flinching. A chocolate-brown spaniel with tan eyebrows and piercing green eyes continued to stare at us. The breeder finally got a nod from "green eyes."

The silence was broken. We were told we were acceptable, and with a sigh of relief, we started to breathe. Air filled our lungs, and we broke into smiles.

The breeder than told us that an older woman had purchased the puppy several weeks ago but had returned him after a week because she was unable to handle the dog's high energy level. Now the dog's lack of kissing (as puppies are known for) made sense. She had loved and had been rejected. She definitely needed a home and love. We had both.

George asked, "What do you intend to call her?"

"SuSu," I said. She is named after a 1942 movie with Ginger Rogers and Ray Milland, *The Major and the Minor*.

We took SuSu home, and gradually that natural puppy love returned. One friend remarked that she had never seen a dog that loved its parents so much.

We miss Annie. We have our memories and remember her special personality. We are also thankful for receiving such a wonderful gift of God's creation, SuSu, our special Christmas gift.

Merry Christmas to you and happy birthday to Jesus.

Susanne, George, Greta, Toni, and SuSu

The Great Chase

Christmas 2013

eorge and SuSu took off for their daily constitutional. As George daydreamed of breaking his record of ten seconds to open a lock, SuSu was experiencing visions of great smells. And was that Mr. Chin's cat, Stucky? Yes, and she had her tail stuck up high, just like her attitude. *I'll show that Stucky*, SuSu thought.

The great chase was on. George lurched forward and out of his daydream and into a world moving too quickly. Stumbling, he lost grip on SuSu's leash.

Now things had revved up to a whole new level. Stucky took off for home with feline speed. She slipped into the lower level and headed for Mr. Chin, who was laying down at the time for a short siesta but soon woke up with the thud of Stucky landing on his chest. As Stucky leaped off, SuSu landed on top of Mr. Chin, knocking him back into a reclining position. SuSu and Stucky went round and round. Mr. Chin went up and down.

In between, George yelled out to Mr. Chin, "Good morning. Sorry to impose. I lost my dog."

I must be losing my mind, Mr. Chin thought with his foggy mind.

"This is serious. Forget your dog."

Stucky and SuSu occasionally darted into other rooms and floors. Making the chase similar to an open house where realtors showed a house up for sale to potential buyers by going through all the rooms. Somehow George was able to secure SuSu's leash and bring the chase to a standstill. Both Stucky and SuSu felt they were the winners with big grins on their faces. George again apologized and said "goodbye" to Mr. Chin, who was once again comatose.

Did I dream this? He was thinking. *But then why is my chest hurting? Odd!* He quickly went back to sleep.

We chase around every day with the demands of life and the need to be on top. It's partly work and partly personal. We need to slow down and smell the poinsettias. Christmas is a time to stop racing. Enjoy its beauty, peace, and goodwill. Merry Christmas.

Susanne, George, SuSu, Greta, and Toni

My View Is Sunny

Christmas 2014

I sat on the Metro bus stop bench on Biscayne Boulevard and looked across the street at the reindeer topography standing at the entrance leading into the Aventura Mall. This brought me to reflect on the season ahead of us. I was thinking of this special time of year and how we reach out in its spirit of unity, peace, and goodwill.

Of course there was the hustle and bustle of shopping and fights over bargain buys. The women sitting next to me on the bench with all those packages had just experienced that stress. I also noticed her looking at my clothes. Her nose seemed to turn up a little. I looked myself over and could see the clothes were a bit worn but clean. I also had a large cloth bag. I pondered, *do I look like a bag lady?*

She looked at my face, which seemed to please her. She moved a little closer toward me, away from the young male boys sitting on the bench. "Did you hear of the robbery in Miami Shores?"

I nodded.

"They robbed the mayor at Starbucks as she sat outside sipping coffee. You don't feel safe anywhere anymore." She clutched her packages and looked over at the two youths sitting next to her.

"I believe the mayor took off after them. Of course, Chief Master and staff responded immediately and caught the culprits. That should make you feel safe." I looked her in the eye and noticed the two youths smirking.

I reached into my bag and offered both her and the two youths a candy cane as the bus arrived. My bus bench friend got first in line. The two youths stepped aside to let me ahead of them. I noticed she acknowledged their manners. She chose an empty seat and sat on the outside toward the aisle to block anyone else from sitting with her. I offered the bus driver a candy cane.

"Good morning, Sunny. Thanks for the candy cane," he replied.

"Hi, Howard." The package lady was stretching her neck to listen to the exchange between the bus driver and myself. She was apparently wondering about my name.

I started to hum a tune. The two youths behind me joined in. Pretty soon everyone was humming, including the lady with the packages. We proceeded down Biscayne Boulevard, humming and smiling. As passengers got off, they smiled at others who were waiting to get on.

I got off at Bayfront Park. The two youths exited with me, along with the package lady. The boys and I sang with the boys' choir of the YMCA at the park. I was lead singer. I had brought candy canes for the choir.

Then a scream rang out. We all ran toward it. Much to my surprise, I found my bus bench lady on the ground rubbing her ankle and yelling that her purse had been stolen.

I spotted an officer who patrolled the park often and called out to him. "Officer O'Brien, over here!"

I also noticed the two youths from the bus run past. The officer was taking her information. Her name was Mrs. Walker, and she lived in a condo building off Brickell Avenue. She declined going to the hospital. She looked a little pale and defeated.

"Officer, I will make sure she gets home safely."

I noticed she looked at me a little suspiciously. I hope I hadn't upset her with this offer. But just then the two youths reappeared and presented Mrs. Walker with her purse. I turned to thank the boys for their fast footwork.

"We will see you tomorrow, Sunny, at the big barbeque."

They smiled.

I then heard Mrs. Walker ask the officer, "Who is that homeless women?" She nodded in my direction.

"Why, that is Sunny. She is not homeless. She tries to break down bias by dressing down. She is highly educated and wealthy." He whistled a happy tune as he left.

The boys formed a seat with their hands. Helpers lifted Mrs. Walker onto the seat. We reached the curb, and immediately a cab appeared. The boys got her settled.

"Where to, Sunny?" the driver asked.

"Thanks for helping, Frank." I gave him the address as well as a candy cane.

Mrs. Walker instructed the driver, "Wait." She looked at me. I saw the white curly hair and the very blues eyes. And yes, she observed my worn clothes. This time she seemed to take in my presence but not judging me by my appearance.

She smiled at me. "I am guilty of judging people by their appearance. I want to apologize. Would you and the boys like to have dinner with me tonight?" She had a hopeful look on her face, which made us all feel equal and welcome.

The boys nodded yes. It didn't matter that we were an odd group. I personally had a Sunny view.

Tis the season to be happy. Share and be at peace!

Susanne, George, Toni, Greta, and SuSu

Dee Dove

Christmas 2015

George and I were looking out our back window at the lake when George jumped up and ran outside. He was yelling, "The vulture has just gotten a baby bird, and the bird has broken free. It is falling, and the vulture is diving after it!"

I raced out after George. I saw him picking up the frightened little bird and cuddling it against his neck. This seemed to calm the baby bird down, but only enraged the vulture. He was now diving for George or rather the baby bird. I ran for some large beach towels in the garage as George headed toward the back stairs.

I started to slap the towel at the bird. I figuratively had George's back. We kept up a speedy walk going up the stairs and slapping the towel toward the vulture. We ran inside and closed the door. There was a big sigh of relief and a little chirp from the baby bird.

After the vulture flew away in defeat, we found a box in the garage that was about the right size to create a little safe bed for the baby bird. As we placed her inside, we noticed she had no tail feathers and assumed they were pulled out as she managed to get away from the vulture. We also noticed the baby was a dove. We put some water and seed for the bird in the box.

George promised me that the next day he would release the bird back outside. I saw the twinkle in his eye as he looked at the dove, and I had reservations that the release may not happen.

Sure enough, the next day when I returned home, I found a new cage with the dove inside. When I questioned George, he said he took the box outside and placed it on a piece of garden furniture by our back window. He opened the top. George went back inside to eat his breakfast, and as he finished, he glanced out the window, only to find the dove perched on the edge of the box watching him. As the day progressed, the bird refused to leave.

George said he was afraid the vulture would return so he brought her inside. He then proceeded to get a nice new cage. He also pointed out that the bird could not fly without her tail feathers and we would have to wait for them to grow back in. I knew deep down that George was delighted with how the events turned out. I was given the honor of naming the bird. It was a natural, Dee Dove!

Dee's tail feathers grew back, but it was never discussed about releasing her. She laid an egg, so we knew the bird was a girl. So we just got her a bigger cage. She is now a part of the household. She has a little bell she rings when she wants something or company. She plays games, answers the phone when she is out flying around the room, and changes the radio station. She hides objects that she sees George working on so they can interact.

Through a frightening experience for Dee, we were able to save her, and she, in turn, gave us her love and gratitude for life. The road in life can be a bumpy one, but along with the jolts, God provides a bigger reward than we would anticipate, a great joy and peace we could only consider a dream. We wish you the experience of God's great love, joy, and peace! Merry Christmas!

Susanne, George, Toni, Greta, Dee, and SuSu

Lucky, the Falling Star

Christmas 2016

Lucky was not really a fallen star. A fallen star can mean that you have done something wrong, like taking an extra cookie when your mom said, "No more." You have then fallen from your mom's good graces or disappointed her.

Now Lucky was really a "falling turtle," a different meaning and spelling. Lucky came falling from the sky. She was not a shooting star either, but a falling turtle.

Let me tell you how this happened: You all know that Santa makes special visits before Christmas to see if you have really been good. Well, this was the day before Christmas Eve, and Santa was in our area with his reindeer. On this trip, he also had some turtles with him because Santa likes to help sick children in need, and he was going to stop by Joe DiMaggio Children's Hospital to bring some joy to those children.

Santa went through a thick cloud cover, which made his sled jump, knocking out a turtle. Santa knew immediately that the turtle had fallen. He told Rudolph to dive and turn around, but as the sled was turning, there was a dove, also called "the bird of peace," flying underneath the sled. If you really took that extra cookie and your mom was mad at you, the dove may whisper in your ear to apologize to your mom. Then your mom would forgive you, and there would be peace again.

Anyway the flying dove had a cousin dove that had been rescued from a big black bird, like a vulture, while flying over our backyard. George had rushed out the back door and caught the dove as it fell from the vulture's grip. I ran outside with a large towel, taking sweeps at the large black bird to keep it away from George and the dove while he brought it inside to safety.

After the dove spent the night, we tried to release it back into the wild, but it had decided that it wanted to stay in our home. We named her Dee Dove.

All the doves in the area would sit on the lines strung from pole to pole on the street in front of our home when they wanted to see Dee. They were happy that she was well taken care of. So the flying dove by Santa's sleigh quickly flew under the falling turtle, and it landed on the dove's back.

Santa was pleased that the turtle was safe and held his sleigh next to the dove as it flew into our backyard and up on the porch. It landed on a small table by our back door. The dove and turtle settled down on to a table, and the dove made sure the turtle was safe in her feathers.

My husband and I were awakened by thundering hooves, jingling bells, and a loud "ho ho ho" as Santa went flying through our backyard. We rushed down to the back door and put on the light.

As we looked out, we saw a dove dip his back feathers to gently slide the turtle on the tabletop. The dove flapped its wings, circled the turtle, and flew away. We opened the door and saw a baby turtle looking at us. We carefully picked it up and brought it inside. The little turtle wagged its little tail. *What a lucky turtle that came to us from the sky*, we thought, and we named it Lucky Star.

We heard another loud noise, and a flock of doves arrived at our back door, all cooing and wanting to get a look at the baby, Lucky Star. Lucky had a happy and peaceful Christmas!

George and I said a thankful prayer for the arrival of our Christmas gift, Lucky Star. All was well in Florida. A Merry Christmas to all!

Susanne, George, Dee, SuSu, Toni, Greta, and Lucky

Love Fest

Christmas 2017

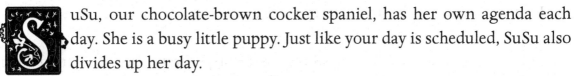

SuSu, our chocolate-brown cocker spaniel, has her own agenda each day. She is a busy little puppy. Just like your day is scheduled, SuSu also divides up her day.

The first category is new friends. SuSu loves to travel to new places. Going bye-bye is always fun, as it gives her a great opportunity to meet new people that she has never seen before. She would qualify for the best Walmart or Home Depot greeter there ever was. Her eyes are always seeking to find new faces entering into her world. It is her mission to say hello to each of them and give them a big wagging of her tail.

Her second mission is to welcome everyone into our and her home. She races to the door to answer the doorbell. New or old friends get welcomed with the same enthusiasm, even if she is having a bad day.

SuSu also paces the day, knowing when all events need to take place. Upon waking, she gets to go outside with her daddy (George). She greets all the children going to school and gets a pat on the head. When lunch rolls around, she likes to eat with us. During the afternoon naptime, SuSu makes sure no one oversleeps into the dinner hour and will promptly wake you up.

Everyone in her family stays together. If one member is not going on an outing, she flat-out refuses to move. She digs in her paws and lays down on the ground until we can convince her there is no problem. No one is forgotten.

The last part of her day is making sure that all the animals under her watch are fed and receive enough food. She will guard their food dishes until they have eaten, making sure another animal does not eat their portion.

Recently a flock of baby ducks were born on our lake. While feeding was taking place, SuSu was terrified that the baby ducks were getting stepped on. She actually cried and whimpered over them with her concern for their safety. SuSu takes great pride in her backyard.

She unfortunately frightens some of her animal friends that see her bounding toward them at great speed. They do not realize she is just happy and wants to play. Greta, the goose with the attitude, has taken to hiding with the flamingo garden statues. Don't believe the saying "bird brain." She stands totally still in a similar pose as the flamingos so SuSu does not recognize her.

A creature of God's love could not do it better. How many of us devote our day to friends, family, neighbors, and animals with the message of God's love, with tail wagging and tongue hanging out? (Maybe it's not a good idea about the tongue hanging out.)

This year bring on the love! Merry Christmas!

Susanne, George, Greta, Dee, Toni, and SuSu

A Cripple

Christmas 2018

Everyone is familiar with Tiny Tim from the famous Scrooge story, *A Christmas Carol*. Our hearts go out to a young child facing the hardship of being crippled. What about a baby bird?

My George spotted a Florida coot with a broken leg and foot. I will refer to him as Tiny Coot. The weather was cooler, and he was feeding Greta, our goose, when he spotted the bird struggling to get some food. Animals do not have the same compassion for weakness in their counterparts as humans do. If they see a weakened fellow bird, they take advantage of the weakness by pushing them out of the way. It is "me first" when food is available.

There was no concern for the crippled little baby bird trying to survive and eat. Fortunately this little bird had a determination of persistence that prevailed over the birds that were not disabled, and he survived. He was able to get enough fallen seeds to stay alive.

When he swam back to the island to sleep for the night, he always swam alone. He went very slowly, and he would have to stop often to regain his strength.

As time went by, George noticed that the bird's broken leg had healed, but his foot was frozen in place. It was shaped like a claw. The bird's spirit was still just as determined. He had to fight for his place to get the scrapes of seed that were left over. George tried to favor him by throwing seed in his direction, away from the other birds, but the other birds were not fooled and only ran toward the new food source, again trying to shut him out. How unchristian is that?

To animals, it is survival of the healthiest. The little coot was not intimidated by their aggression toward him. Now Tiny Coot used his claw foot as a weapon to defend himself from their greed, and he raised the claw foot and charged. The other birds were now intimidated by him and backed away, allowing Tiny Coot to eat alongside them. He was now accepted. He still swam alone, but now his crippled foot acted like a paddle and helped him get to the island without having to stop and rest.

God kept Tiny Coot's hope alive. God loved him and watched over him. God did not overburden Tiny Coot with what he could not overcome. We all face challenges. It is important to know that God is there to offer the hope and love to help with our burdens. God is involved with our problems, just like he is with those of the little bird. Christmas is a beautiful time to enjoy God's love and share this adoration with our family, friends, neighbors, or strangers who cross our path. Merry Christmas.

Susanne, George, Greta, Toni, Dee, and SuSu (who sends her love)

Memories

Some of my favorite memories of Christmas are as following, but not necessarily in this order:

- Christmas cookies baking (my daughter is better at this than I am)
- The smell of a live Christmas tree
- Christmas cards
- Candy canes
- Christmas lights
- The gathering of family, neighbors, and friends in the spirit of sharing love, joy, and giving (presents)
- Christmas wreaths
- Snow angels
- Christmas carols
- Christmas church services
- Charity giving
- The spirit of goodwill, which is more pronounced
- The cross, star, angel, wise men, and the manger
- The great Christmas story

Printed in the United States
By Bookmasters